BATMAN
DISCARD

NIGHTMARE IN GOTHAM CITY

by
Donald Lemke

illustrated by
Andie Tong

Batman created by Bob Kane

HARPER FESTIVAL
An Imprint of HarperCollinsPublishers

HarperFestival is an imprint of HarperCollins Publishers.

Batman: Nightmare in Gotham City
Copyright © 2015 DC Comics.
BATMAN and all related characters and elements are trademarks of and © DC Comics.
(s15)

HARP33058
Manufactured in China.
ISBN 978-0-06-234486-1

Book design by Victor Joesph Ochoa
15 16 17 18 19 SCP 10 9 8 7 6 5 4 3 2 1

❖
First Edition

BATMAN

Orphaned as a child, young Bruce Wayne trained his body and mind to become Batman, the Dark Knight. Using high-tech gadgets and weapons, Batman fights against the most dangerous criminals in Gotham City.

COMMISSIONER JAMES GORDON

James Gordon is the Gotham City Police Commissioner. He works with Batman to stop crime in the city.

SCARECROW

At Gotham University, Professor Jonathan Crane experimented with fear. Later he became Scarecrow, a frightful super-villain. His fear toxin makes people's worst nightmares come to life.

On Halloween night, a bright orange moon shines down on Gotham City. Hundreds of people gather for the opening of a haunted house. The event will raise money for the city's police department.

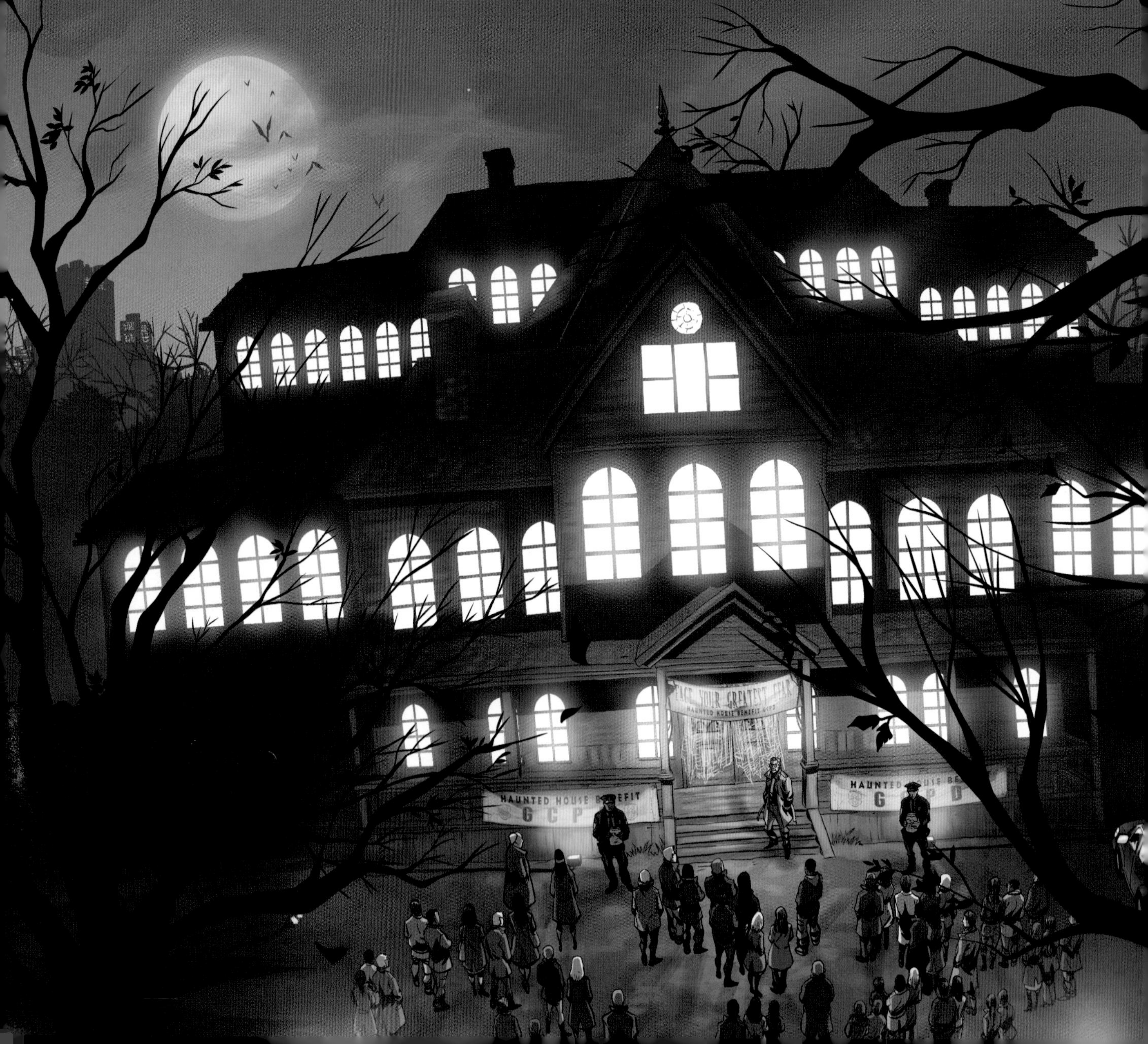
FACE YOUR GREATEST FEAR

Police Commissioner James Gordon steps onto the creaky front porch. "Welcome, everyone!" he says to the visitors. "Are you ready to . . . Face Your Greatest Fear?"

WOOOOH! A ghoulish howl echoes from the haunted house. The porch lights flicker and flash. Mechanical skeletons rattle to life on the front lawn.

"Don't be afraid," Gordon tells the crowd. "Tonight, this house is the safest place in Gotham City." He points to other police officers working at the event. "Now step inside," the commissioner adds, opening the front door, "if you dare!"

The crowd funnels into the haunted house. They twist and turn through the dark hallways. Actors dressed as zombies, monsters, and ghosts jump out at them.

Soon the first visitors reach a narrow stairwell to the second floor. At the top stands a shadowy figure in a long black coat. "Who are you supposed to be?" a visitor asks him. "Your worst nightmare!" replies Scarecrow.

POOF! The gas spills through the hallways like a rushing river. Guests cough, choke, and fall to their knees. "Now that's what I call a chemical reaction!" says Scarecrow with a laugh.

Scarecrow's fear toxin brings nightmares to life. People flee the haunted house, swatting at imaginary spiders, rats, and snakes.

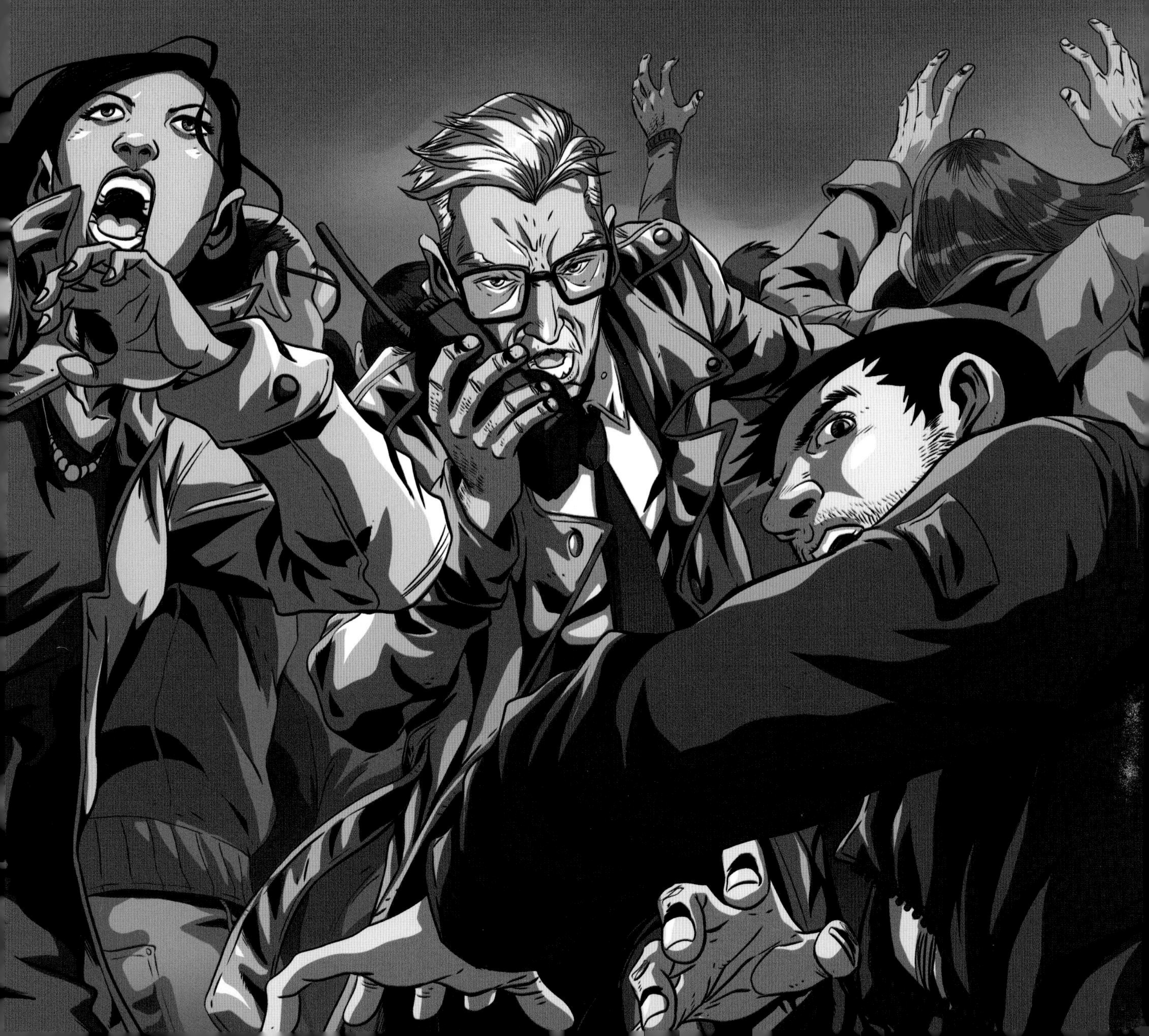

Moments later, Batman arrives in the Batmobile. "I'm afraid someone has taken over the haunted house," Gordon tells the Dark Knight.

"Do not fear, Commissioner," Batman says, smirking. "This trickster is in for a treat."

Stepping inside, Batman flips on his night-vision goggles. The high-tech device lets him see in the dark. All around him, people scream in fright. They smash and break whatever they can grab.

Suddenly a man with green hair and an evil grin sprints past Batman. "The Joker," the super hero says.

Batman removes the grapnel gun from his Utility Belt. He spins and fires an ultra-thin wire at the villain's ankles.

The Joker trips and hits the floor with a *THUD*! Batman kneels next to the criminal, but the fallen man isn't the Joker after all. He's an actor in a Halloween mask!

"Looks like the joke's on you," says a voice from behind. Batman turns, spotting the real villain.
"Scarecrow," growls the Dark Knight, "I thought you'd be behind this crime."

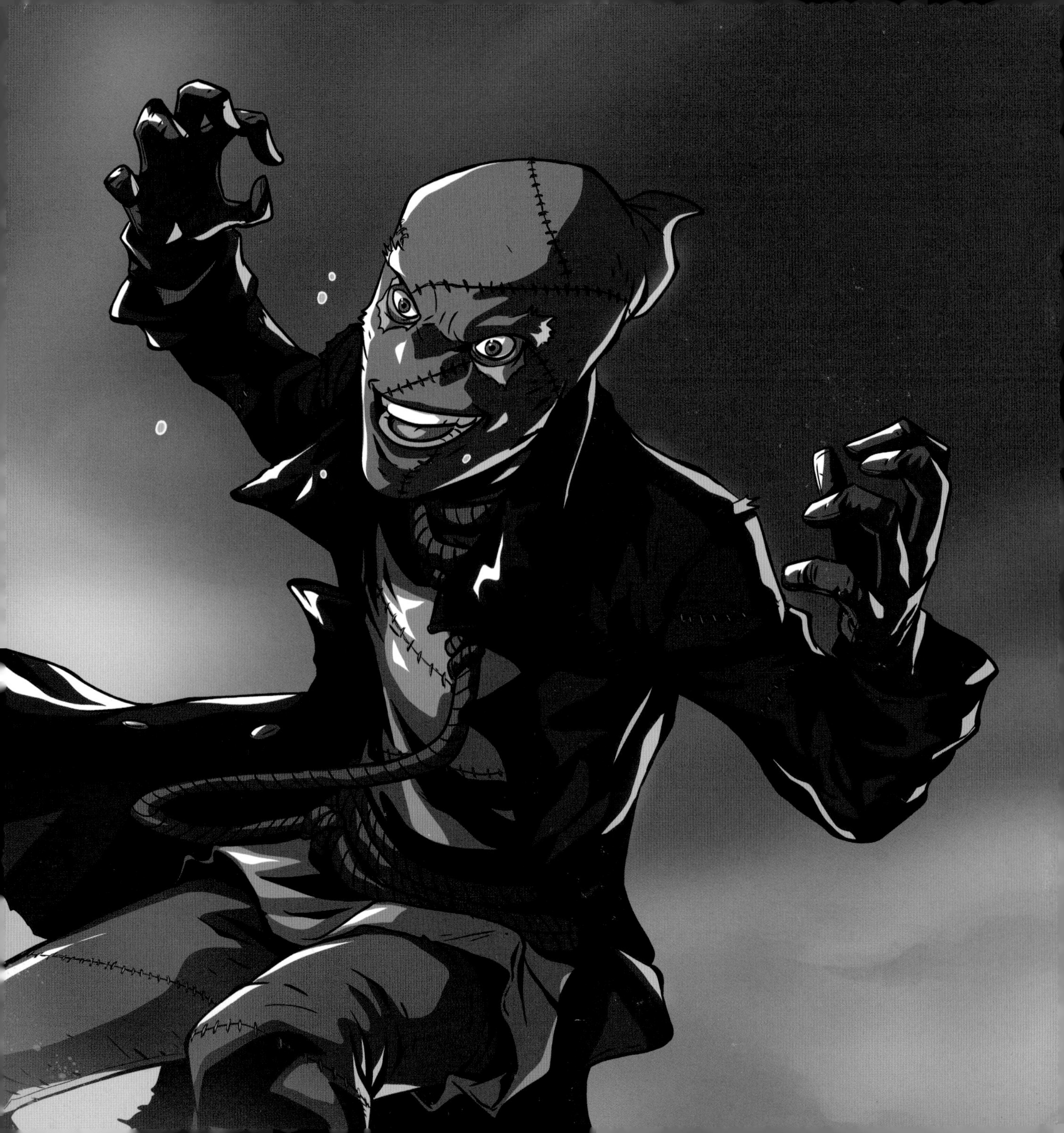

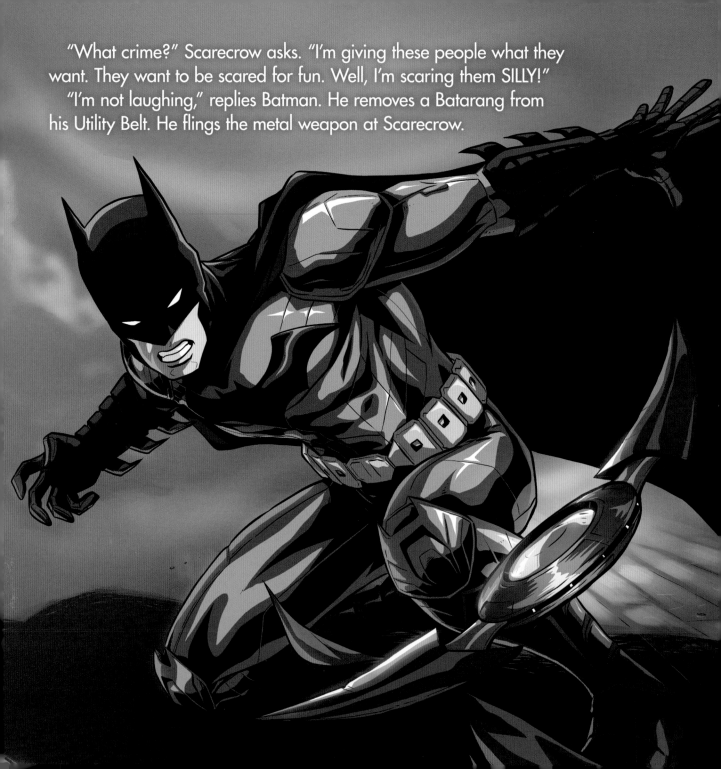

"What crime?" Scarecrow asks. "I'm giving these people what they want. They want to be scared for fun. Well, I'm scaring them SILLY!"

"I'm not laughing," replies Batman. He removes a Batarang from his Utility Belt. He flings the metal weapon at Scarecrow.

The frightful villain ducks into a nearby hallway. *CLANG!*
The Batarang sticks into a wall as Scarecrow escapes.
Batman chases the fleeing villain. The halls are filled with
frightened visitors.

Batman follows Scarecrow into the basement of the haunted house.
The villain stands near the cellar door, holding a silver can in his hand.

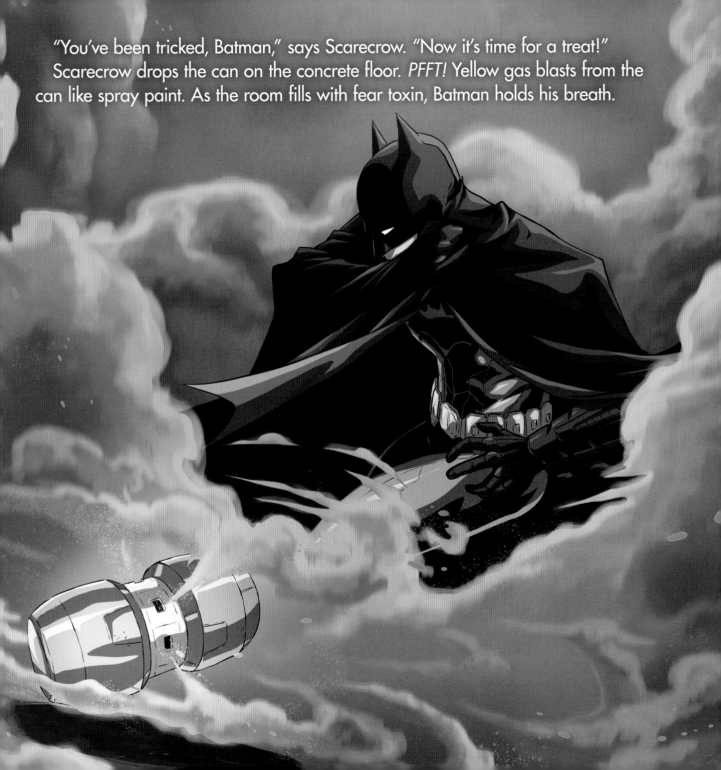

"You've been tricked, Batman," says Scarecrow. "Now it's time for a treat!" Scarecrow drops the can on the concrete floor. *PFFT!* Yellow gas blasts from the can like spray paint. As the room fills with fear toxin, Batman holds his breath.

Scarecrow reaches for the cellar door. "Have a good fright!" he says, pushing on the door to escape. It's locked. *WHAM! WHAM!* The villain pounds on the door in panic. "OPEN!" he screams.

Batman puts on his gas mask. Fresh air flows into the hero's lungs, and he starts breathing again. "What's the matter?" asks Batman. "Scared?"

An hour later, the doors of the haunted house swing open. The effect of Scarecrow's fear toxin has worn off. People laugh and smile.

"Wow!" says one guest. "That's the best haunted house I've ever visited!"

"Me too!" agrees another. Everyone happily gives money to the police department.

At last, Batman exits the house with Scarecrow in handcuffs. Commissioner Gordon greets them. "Nice work," he tells the super hero.

"You, too," Batman replies.

"Isn't it funny how people want to be scared sometimes?" Gordon asks.

"Yes," Batman replies, "but nobody should *have* to be afraid." The hero turns and then adds, "Except for the criminals, of course."

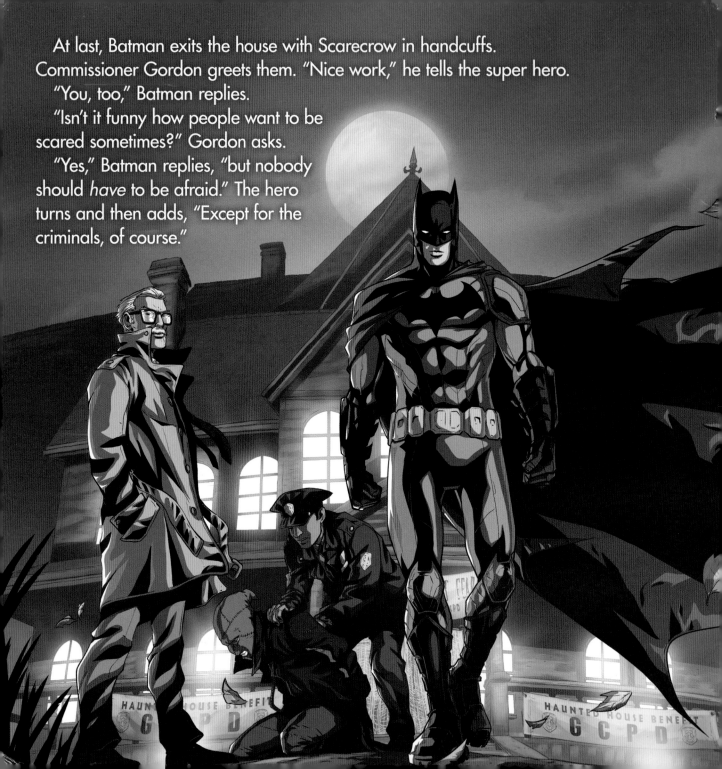